We Love Holidays
DIVALI

Saviour Pirotta

PowerKiDS
press

New York

Saviour Pirotta is a highly experienced author, who has written many books for young children. He was born in Malta and is also a trained chef.

Published in 2008 by The Rosen Publishing Group, Inc.
29 East 21st Street, New York, NY 10010

First Edition

The publishers would like to thank the following for allowing us to reproduce their pictures in this book:

Alamy: 6, Ark Religion; 8, 12. Fabrice Bettex; 9, Dinodia Images; 10, Robert Holmes; 13, Paul Gapper; 15, Yograj Jadeja; 16, Paul Doyle; 17, World Religions; 23, David Sanger Photography / aargee stationers: 5 / Christine Osbourne: 14 / Corbis: 22, Jayanta Shaw, Reuters; 4, Lindsay Hebberd; 19, John Slater; 18, Najlah Feanny / Thirdangle: cover, 7, 11 / Getty Images: 20, AFP / Art Directors: 21, Helene Rogers.

Library of Congress Cataloging-in-Publication Data

Pirotta, Saviour.
  Divali / Saviour Pirotta. -- 1st ed.
     p. cm. -- (We love holidays)
  Includes index.
  ISBN-13: 978-1-4042-3706-3
  ISBN-10: 1-4042-3706-2 (library binding)
  1. Divali--Juvenile literature. I. Title.
  BL1239.82.D58P57 2007
  294.5'36--dc22
                                        2006026793

Manufactured in China

Contents

The festival of lights

Welcome to Divali, the festival of light and happiness. It's time to clean your house. It's time to buy new clothes and stock up on sweets. And don't forget to send Divali cards to your friends.

These people are decorating their house for Divali. ▼

Divali takes place over five days in October and November. It is the biggest festival of the Hindu year. Sikhs and **Jains** celebrate Divali too.

Divali ▲ (or Diwali) cards tell your friends you are thinking of them.

DID YOU KNOW?

Divali takes place in the Hindu months of Ashwin and Kartik.

Rama and Sita

During Divali, people from Northern India celebrate the return of King Rama and his bride, Princess Sita, to their kingdom. Rama's followers lit thousands of lamps to show Rama and Sita the way.

The demon ▶ king **Ravana** had kidnapped Sita. In this picture Rama is fighting him to save her.

▲
These children
have lit Divali
lamps to show
that light wins
over darkness.

Today, people still light lamps or candles at Divali to remember the holy king and his princess bride.

DID YOU KNOW?

Monkeys also helped
Rama and Sita to escape
from Ravana.

Welcome, goddess

Some houses in England are lit up for Divali. ▶

Divali lights are also lit to invite the goddess **Lakshmi** into people's homes. Lakshmi is the goddess of wealth. A visit from her means good luck for the whole year.

HAPPY DIVALI

8

◄ Lanterns are covered in colorful paper and decorations.

Lamps and candles are placed in windows, outside houses, and on roofs. Even stores, offices, garages, and streets are decorated with Divali lamps. People know that Lakshmi will visit the houses with the brightest lights.

Patterns by the door

To welcome Lakshmi and visitors, children help to draw **Rangoli** patterns by their front door. Most Rangoli patterns are made of colored sand or rice powder mixed with water.

The white paste used to make these patterns stands for **purity.** ▼

They include pictures of birds, flowers, stars, moons, and gods. Many draw pictures of tiny footsteps, too. These show that Lakshmi has visited the house.

These ▲ children are drawing Rangoli patterns with colored paints.

11

A prayer for Lakshmi

This statue of Lakshmi has been decorated with flowers. ▶

People set up a special **altar** for Lakshmi in their homes. They decorate it with flowers, lights, and sometimes coins. Children sing special songs at the altar.

The grown-ups pray that Lakshmi will bring them luck in the coming year. All through the festival, people leave their windows open, so that Lakshmi can come into their house.

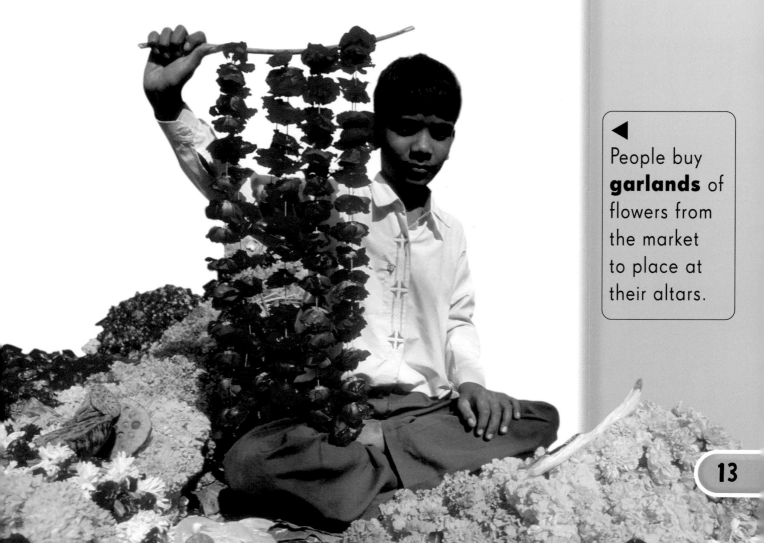

◄ People buy **garlands** of flowers from the market to place at their altars.

Lights in the sky

Divali is the celebration of light. The burning lamps remind people to thank the gods for all they have. Everyone celebrates good winning over evil and light winning over darkness.

Children have fun with sparklers on Divali night. ▶

14

Sparklers and firecrackers are set off.
In many cities, there are huge
fireworks displays.

In some countries, they have Divali fireworks for many nights.

DID YOU KNOW?

People think that the noisy fireworks remind the gods that the people are happy and thankful.

A time for sharing

Divali is a time for sharing good food. People spend days preparing sweets and snacks to eat with their friends and family. Round and square sweets decorated with nuts and raisins are very popular.

Children also have a special Divali porridge with rice or **sago**. Divali dinner is often a vegetarian curry. The different vegetables in it remind people of a good **harvest**.

Everyone brings food to the **temple** altar for the gods and for each other. ▼

Happy New Year

The day after Divali is New Year's Day. It is a time of new beginnings. Everyone wears new clothes. Families visit friends and relatives and exchange presents. Children touch the feet of grown up relatives to get blessings and money.

Families and friends get together and enjoy the celebrations. ▶

People buy new things for their house. It's lucky to spend some money on New Year's Day.

DID YOU KNOW?

People pay back money they have borrowed, enemies make up, and farmers sow new crops.

Sikh Divali

For Sikhs, Divali is a double celebration. The first stone of the Golden Temple in Amritsar, the holy Sikh city, was laid on Divali many years ago.

Many people come to see the Golden Temple lit up for Divali. ▼

It was also on Divali that a Sikh leader, Guru Hargobind Sahib, was released from prison. His followers covered the Golden Temple with lights to welcome him back. Ever since, Sikhs have celebrated Divali in his honor.

Guru Hargobind Sahib was a famous Sikh leader. ◄

sister and brother

The last day of the Divali festival is a special day for brothers and sisters. Sisters cook their brothers' favorite dishes. They place a red dot, a tilak, on their brothers' forehead.

Bengali women pray for their brothers on the last day of Divali.
▼

In return, their brothers give them nice presents. They bless them, too. It's a wonderful end to the festival of light and joy. Everyone looks forward to Divali again next year.

◄ A tilak like this one is thought to protect a person from harm.

Index

Glossary

altar a surface used for making offerings to a god or goddess

garlands wreaths of flowers worn or hung up for decoration

harvest the gathering of crops

Jain an Indian religion

Lakshmi the Hindu goddess of wealth

purity pureness and cleanliness

rangoli sacred patterns that are painted outside houses and temples

Ravana the many-headed demon king from the Hindu Ramayana

sago a starchy food made from the sago palm, used in puddings

temple a building used for the worship of a god or gods

tilak a dot placed on the forehead, thought to protect men from harm